A **Rookie** reader® •

09-BHJ-738

3 4028 07704 5668
HARRIS COUNTY PUBLIC LIBRARY

JPIC Rockli
Rockliff, Mara
Next to an ant

LAP

$5.95
ocn694283168
11/17/2011

WITHDRAWN

Next to an Ant

Written by Mara Rockliff
Illustrated by Pascale Constantin

Children's Press®
A Division of Scholastic Inc.
New York • Toronto • London • Auckland • Sydney
Mexico City • New Delhi • Hong Kong
Danbury, Connecticut

Dear Parents/Educators,

Welcome to Rookie Ready to Learn. Each Rookie Reader in this series includes additional age-appropriate Let's Learn Together activity pages that help your young child to be better prepared when starting school. *Next to an Ant* offers opportunities for you and your child to talk about the important social/emotional skill of **self-awareness**.

Here are early-learning skills you and your child will encounter in the *Next to an Ant* Let's Learn Together pages:

• Self-awareness
• Understanding and comparing sizes
• Colors
• Prepositions

We hope you enjoy sharing this delightful, enhanced reading experience with your early learner.

Library of Congress Cataloging-in-Publication Data

Rockliff, Mara.
  Next to an ant / written by Mara Rockliff ; illustrated by Pascale Constantin.
    p. cm. -- (Rookie ready to learn)
  Summary: A child compares the size of various items and discovers that she is the tallest of all. Includes suggested learning activities.

  ISBN 978-0-531-26447-8 — ISBN 978-0-531-26747-9 (pbk.)

  [1. Size--Fiction.] I. Constantin, Pascale, ill. II. Title. III. Series
  PZ7.R5887Ne 2011
  [E]--dc22
                        2010049993

© 2011 by Scholastic Inc.
Illustrations © 2011 Pascale Constantin
All rights reserved.
Printed in the United States of America. 113

CHILDREN'S PRESS, and ROOKIE READY TO LEARN, and associated logos are trademarks and or registered trademarks of Scholastic Library Publishing. SCHOLASTIC and associated logos are trademarks or registered trademarks of Scholastic, Inc.

1 2 3 4 5 6 7 8 9 10 R 18 17 16 15 14 13 12 11

Next to an ant,
a berry is tall.

Next to a berry,
a snail is tall.

Next to a snail,
a mouse is tall.

Next to a mouse,
my shoe is tall.

Next to my shoe,
my cup is tall.

Next to my cup,
my ball is tall.

Next to my ball,
my basket is tall.

Next to my basket,
my puppy is tall.

Next to my puppy,
my brother is tall.

And I?

I am the tallest one of all!

Congratulations!

You just finished reading
Next to an Ant and
learned all about size.

About the Author
Next to an ant, Mara Rockliff is very tall indeed. She lives in
Charlottesville, Virginia, with her family.

About the Illustrator
After many years as a sculptor, Pascale Constantin discovered a
passion for illustration. Fantastic creatures and funny characters
jump from her brushes onto the paper as if by magic.

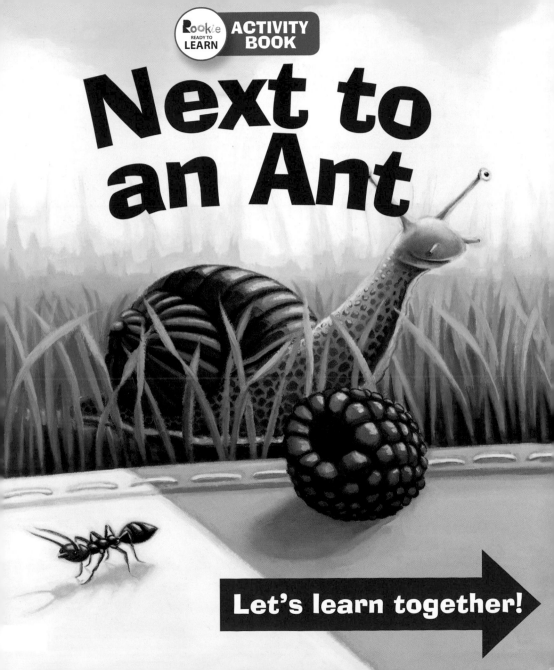

The Ants Go Marching

(Sing this song to the tune of "The Ants Go Marching.")

The ants go marching one by one,
hurrah, hurrah.
The ants go marching one by one,
hurrah, hurrah.
The ants go marching one by one,
The little one stops to suck his thumb.
And they all go marching
down to the ground
To get out of the rain,
BOOM! BOOM! BOOM!

(Sing three verses of this
song. Change *one by one* to
two by two and sing *The little
one stops to tie his shoe*. Then
change *two by two* to *three by
three* and sing *The little one
stops to climb a tree*.)

Big and Small

The girl in the book went on a picnic. She saw things that were different sizes. Help her decide which things were bigger and which were smaller. You can answer each question by pointing to the correct picture.

Which is bigger?

tree

berry

Which is smaller?

dog

ant

Which is bigger?

glass

ball

PARENT TIP: This activity helps children identify the difference between big and small. Explain to your child that there are other words for *big*, such as *tall* and *large*, and other words for *small*, such as *little* and *tiny*.

Where Is the Animal?

The animals went exploring after the picnic. Where did each one go? Read this rhyming story to find out.

The  **ant** is **under** the **plant**.

The **mouse** is **next** to the **house**.

The **snail** is **on** the **pail**.

The **dog** is **behind** the **log**.

PARENT TIP: You can help your child understand position words during playtime or everyday activities. For instance, while bouncing a ball, discuss when the ball goes up or down. You may also want to play a simple "I Spy" game, using position words. For example, say "I spy something blue that is behind something red."

28

Colors Everywhere

The girl and her brother went on a picnic. There were many things to see. Look closely at this picnic picture.

1. Point to and name ⬤ things you see in the picture.
   green

2. Point to and name ⬤ things you see in the picture.
   yellow

3. Point to and name ⬤ things you see in the picture.
   blue

PARENT TIP: Being outside is a great opportunity to point out colors to your child. Next time you go on a walk, search for different colors in nature.

What's the Opposite?

When they are next to each other, the brother is tall and the puppy is short. *Tall* and *short* are opposites.

Say each word in the top row. Then point to the word that is its opposite.

big

hot

full

empty

little

cold

PARENT TIP: Identifying opposites helps build children's problem-solving skills. Encourage your child to act out different opposites through body movement, such as *up/down, happy/sad, loud/quiet, in/out, high/low, stop/go,* and *open/close.*